Big Island
Search

backpack mysteries

Too Many Treasures
Big Island Search

9607

a backpack mystery

Big Island
Search

Mary Carpenter Reid

BETHANY HOUSE PUBLISHERS
MINNEAPOLIS, MINNESOTA 55438

Big Island Search
Copyright © 1996
Mary Carpenter Reid

Cover and story illustrations by Paul Turnbaugh.

Published by Bethany House Publishers
A Ministry of Bethany Fellowship, Inc.
11300 Hampshire Avenue South
Minneapolis, Minnesota 55438

Printed in the United States of America.

Library of Congress Cataloging-in-Publication Data

Reid, Mary.
    Big Island search / Mary Carpenter Reid.
       p.   cm. — (A Backpack mystery ; 2)
    Summary: While staying with their mother's cousin Jangles on an estate on
the island of Hawaii, Steff and her sister Paulie are determined to find a
missing artifact in order to save Jangles' job.
    ISBN 1–55661–716–X
    [1. Mystery and detective stories. 2. Hawaii—Fiction. 3. Christian life—
Fiction.] I. Title. II. Series: Reid, Mary.
Backpack mystery ; 2.
PZ7.R2727Bi   1996
[Fic]—dc20
96–25226   CIP
AC

To Clinton—
a great person
in my family.

MARY CARPENTER REID loves to visit places just like the places Steff and Paulie visit. Does she stay with peculiar relatives? That's her secret!

She will tell you her family is wonderful. She likes reading and writing children's books. She likes colors and computers. She especially likes getting letters from her readers.

She can't organize things as well as Steff does, but she makes lots of lists.

Two cats—a calico cat and a tiger cat—live at her house in California. *They* are very peculiar!

contents

1. Best Job in the World 9

2. Mr. Franklin's Thing-u-ma-jig 15

3. Missing Pages 20

4. Trigg and Reef Join the Team 24

5. Hidden Sidewalk 29

6. The Water Clue 35

7. Visitors on the Ceiling.................. 38

8. Quitters 42

9. In the Lava Tube 47

10. Flashing Sign 52

11. Way to Go, Jangles! 56

12. Clue Review 61

13. Cast-Iron Message 66

14. Our Search Team Never Quits 71

Let us not become weary in doing good.

Galatians 6:9

best job in the world

"Wow! Cousin Jangles, you must have the best job in the world," Steff Larson told the man driving the car.

"Yes," said her younger sister, Paulie. "You get to live in Hawaii."

Steff added, "On an estate."

Paulie said, "And it's free."

"He is the manager," Steff told her. "That's why it's free."

Paulie said, "I already know he is the manager. He takes care of a fancy house and lots of land."

"You girls are right," said Jangles. "I do have the best job in the world. I just wish . . ."

Steff waited for him to finish the sentence. He didn't.

In fact, he had said very little on the long, dark drive from the airport.

Steff sighed. It was awfully hard having to stay with relatives so often.

She and Paulie and their parents had flown across the ocean to Honolulu that day.

Steff's mother and father had remained in Honolulu. They put the girls on a second, smaller airplane. The smaller plane brought Steff and Paulie to the island where their mother's Cousin Jangles lived—the Big Island of Hawaii.

Their father had told them, "Your mom and I will be working all the time we are here in Honolulu. It is important to our business. You would not like sitting around the hotel by yourselves."

Their mother promised, "You girls will have

fun staying with my Cousin Jangles. And you'll like his new wife, Marsha."

Steff hoped so.

But something seemed to be bothering Jangles.

The car turned in to a driveway. The headlights flashed over plants of all sizes growing on both sides.

"Oooh, look at the flowers!" Paulie exclaimed. "Steff, let's make flower necklaces."

"Maybe we can find orchids. An orchid lei would be great."

Ahead stood a large white house. Light glowed from many windows. Steps led up to a wide porch.

The car stopped. The girls threw their backpacks over their shoulders. Jangles carried everything else.

Inside the house, Jangles' wife, Marsha, hugged the girls. She kissed her husband on the cheek.

She showed him a sheet of paper. "This FAX message came from Mr. Franklin. You are to meet him at the airport at eleven o'clock Saturday morning."

Jangles slapped a hand to his forehead and groaned. "That means it is going to happen."

Paulie looked at Steff and mouthed a question, "*It?*"

Steff didn't know what *it* was.

Jangles read from the FAX. " 'The History Group will come to the estate at noon. I will give them the artifact in a short ceremony. I have not been there for many years, but I know you will have the estate in tip-top shape. Of course, please be sure the artifact is dry and clean.' "

Jangles crumpled the paper. "Artifact!" he exploded. "Why can't Mr. Franklin ever say what the artifact is?"

Marsha frowned and tilted her head toward Steff and Paulie.

Jangles blinked as if he had forgotten they were there. Quickly he said, "Not a biggie! Just a message from the boss—the man who owns this place."

Marsha told the girls, "Let's telephone your

parents and tell them you got here safely. Then we'll have cookies and papaya."

"What's *pa-pah-ya*?" asked Paulie.

"Delicious, creamy, yellow fruit," answered Marsha.

They all sat at the kitchen table.

Paulie tasted a bite of fruit between bites of cookie.

Steff liked the papaya better than the cookie.

Jangles liked both. He ate and ate.

Outside, a breeze rustled palm branches. Warm air danced through the open windows carrying sweet smells of flowers.

Steff said again, "Cousin Jangles, you must have the best job in the world."

He said, "Yep. At least until Saturday."

Steff was afraid to ask more about Saturday. Mr. Franklin was coming. Was that so terrible?

2

Mr. franklin's thing-u-ma-jig

Marsha helped the girls get settled in their room.

After she left, Paulie got into one of the twin beds and said her prayers. Steff took a book from her backpack and crawled into the other bed. She started reading.

Everything was quiet until Paulie asked, "Steff, remember when Jangles came to visit our house? He laughed a lot."

"Yes, he did," Steff said. "I guess he didn't

feel like laughing tonight. But don't worry. I know he likes us."

"Remember when Jangles told us he got his name because his beads jingled and jangled?"

Steff said, "He still wears those silver beads."

"He doesn't dress like Dad."

Jangles dressed in sparkling white jeans and Hawaiian shirts.

Paulie's voice began to sound wobbly. "And his hair is longer than Dad's hair."

Jangles' hair was long and curly and gray.

Steff put away her book and turned off the light. "Jesus doesn't mind that Jangles does not dress or talk like most other people we know."

Just when Steff thought Paulie had finally gone to sleep, Paulie whispered, "I wish Mom and Dad didn't have to go on trips for the business."

Figuring out what to say wasn't always easy when you were the big sister. But Steff was sure her mother loved and trusted Cousin Jangles. She told Paulie, "It's OK to be here."

In the kitchen the next morning, Jangles set the table for three. "Marsha has classes every

day. She is learning to work in a medical office."
He put out cereal boxes. "Take your pick."

"I'll have the cocoa cereal, please," said Paulie.

She always chose cocoa.

"Cool!" said Jangles.

Steff nibbled on toast.

She decided it would be OK to ask Jangles a question. "Cousin Jangles . . . uh . . . are you going to get fired from this job?"

Paulie's spoon stopped halfway to her mouth.

Jangles spread guava jelly on his toast. "I will unless I can find Mr. Franklin's artifact by Saturday." Jangles pushed the jelly close to the edges. "Last night you probably guessed that I had hoped his plans would change or something. But Mr. Franklin is coming Saturday to give his artifact to the History Group."

Jangles drew a big breath and puffed it out slowly. "And that's a fact."

Paulie giggled. "*Art-i-fact* and *that's-a-fact.* You made a rhyme."

Jangles grinned. "How about that? *Art-i-fact*

and *that's-a-fact*! Nice touch, huh?"

Then Paulie asked, "What is an artifact?"

"An artifact is something made by people," answered Jangles. "Usually it's something historical."

"What is Mr. Franklin's artifact?" asked Paulie.

"I wish I knew."

Steff could not believe what she was hearing. "You're supposed to get something ready for a ceremony on Saturday and you don't know what it is? Or where it is?"

Jangles waved his knife. "Nope. Bummer, don't you think?"

"That's not fair! Mr. Franklin should have told you."

"He probably did tell me that day on the mainland when he hired me. I guess I didn't catch everything he said. I was too excited about getting this job."

Paulie said, "Call him on the telephone. Ask him."

Steff had been about to say the same thing.

That was before she saw the shocked look on Jangles' face.

She told her sister, "Things aren't that simple, Paulie."

Jangles pretended to hold a telephone to his ear. "I could call Mr. Franklin. I could say, Mr. Franklin, I have been taking good care of everything on your estate for six months. By the way, what and where is your precious thing-u-ma-jig?"

Paulie laughed.

"Well," Steff said, "you *do* know that whatever it is needs to be dry and clean."

"Oh, I know more than that. Follow me."

3

MISSING PAGES

Jangles led the way from the kitchen past several rooms. One was a library.

Paulie grabbed Steff. "If he gets fired on Saturday, what about us?"

"Shhh!"

Jangles stopped at a room with a desk. "This is my office," he said, "for a few more days."

He took sheets of paper from a drawer. "Mr. Franklin sent these messages on the FAX machine. Trouble is, the machine doesn't always print out everything."

Steff asked, "You mean, parts of what Mr. Franklin sends are missing?"

"Sometimes whole pages. A guy checked the machine. Didn't find anything wrong. He thinks it might be the humidity."

Steff explained to Paulie, "The damp air."

Jangles tapped his chest with his thumb. "Actually, I'm afraid I might cause some of the problem. I know about gardening, but I haven't been around office machines much."

He flipped through the pages. "In this FAX, Mr. Franklin says the artifact has been on the estate for many years. Here, he tells me to build a strong crate for moving the artifact to town."

"Must be heavy," said Paulie.

"Listen to this," Jangles said. " 'It played an important part in the history of the Islands. School children will visit it.' "

Jangles slammed the papers on the desk. "I should have told him long ago that I don't know what the artifact is. I kept thinking I'd find out."

"Could you tell him you didn't get all the FAX pages?" asked Steff.

Jangles squirmed. "Mr. Franklin thinks I'm a good manager. I *am*. I'm really good with plants! And I'm good at growing special vegetables and figuring out which ones do best in this soil. He trusts me to handle his estate. I don't like to say I can't even handle his FAX machine."

Paulie touched Jangles' arm. "I hope you don't get fired."

"Me too," Jangles said. "This is my first real job, you know. Maybe your mom told you girls that I used to mostly surf and hang out at the beach and not work much."

Steff had heard her mother say only that Jangles was creative and a little different.

Jangles brightened. "Last year, I went on my knees to Jesus. He forgave me and helped me get my act together. Then Mr. Franklin hired me. Then Marsha married me."

"Wow!" said Steff.

She studied the FAX messages. How could she and Paulie help?

Jangles snapped his fingers. "Yep, everything has been cool lately. Except this artifact thing. Bummer."

The messages were mostly about soil and vegetables and bills. Steff looked for ones about the artifact.

Suddenly, Steff knew what to do.

She cried, "These messages are filled with clues."

Paulie said, "Like a mystery!"

Jangles said, "It *is* a mystery."

Steff told Jangles, "Paulie and I will organize a search team. We will search the estate."

"Search team. Cool!" said Jangles. "That's nice of you girls. Thanks. However, I work all over the estate. I keep looking as I work, and I haven't seen anything that could be Mr. Franklin's artifact."

But Steff was already sorting the messages into stacks. "We will find it—whatever it is."

Paulie told Jangles, "My sister likes to organize things."

4

trigg and reef join the team

Steff set up search team headquarters at a table in the library.

"We need a map," she said.

Jangles brought a rolled-up paper from his office and spread it on the table.

"Here's an old drawing of the estate. It shows buildings, sidewalks, and fences."

Steff pointed to a large circle a little way from the house. "What's that?" she asked.

"Might have been a big flower bed," said

Jangles. "Remember, this drawing is old. The estate may look very different now."

From outside the window came voices.

Two boys about Steff's age walked up the driveway.

Jangles called, "Hey, Trigg! Hey, Reef! Meet us on the porch."

Jangles told Steff and Paulie, "Those boys live nearby. They help me some mornings. Kind of junior gardeners."

On the porch, he introduced them.

"You guys talk a few minutes. Then come on down to the garden shack."

Steff and Paulie sat on the top step.

Steff said, "You pull weeds and stuff?"

"Yes, and help in Jangles' vegetable gardens," answered Trigg. "He knows more about plants than anybody."

"What do you do for fun?"

Trigg said, "Ride bikes."

Reef spoke up. "We have a club."

"Neat," said Steff. "What kind?"

Trigg jabbed Reef with an elbow.

Reef said quickly, "It's our own club. We do stuff . . . by ourselves."

Trigg said, "He means, our club is for guys only."

Steff suddenly had an idea. "Paulie and I have a team."

"What kind of a team?" asked Trigg.

"A search team. We are searching the estate."

"For what?"

"A missing artifact." She explained what an artifact was.

"Why do you have to search for it?" Trigg asked.

"We don't know exactly where it is."

Paulie rolled her eyes and said, "We don't know exactly *what* it is."

Steff gave her a stern look. "We have a map and clues."

"It's a mystery," Paulie said.

"A mystery?" Reef acted interested.

"What kind of clues?" asked Trigg.

Paulie said, "School kids will visit the artifact."

Reef made a face. "Field trips."

"We have more clues than that," said Steff. "Do you want to help us search?"

Trigg said, "It would be hard to find anything out of doors. Around here, plants grow really fast and big and close together. You have to keep cutting them back. Except where it is too rocky."

"Ever been to Hawaii before?" asked Reef.

"No," answered Steff.

Reef grinned at Trigg. "Mainland girls. Probably never seen a gecko."

"A what?" asked Paulie.

Steff said, "Do you want to be on our search team or not?"

Trigg looked at Reef. "Sure."

"Might as well," said Reef.

Paulie asked, "What's a gecko?"

Trigg said, "We work with Jangles mornings."

Reef added, "We'll come after lunch."

The boys went toward the garden shack.

Paulie said, "Hey, they didn't tell us what a gecko is!"

5

hidden sidewalk

The girls went into the house.

Steff wrote down the clues and made a copy for everyone.

CLUES ABOUT THE ARTIFACT

Should be dry and clean.
Heavy. Needs strong crate for trip to town.
Old. Been on estate for many years.
Useful for school field trips.
Played important part in history of Islands.

Steff told Paulie the plan. "You and I will search inside the house and buildings. We will search outside when Trigg and Reef are helping."

Paulie said, "Let's search the house now."

"Wait! It's important to get organized before we begin," Steff said. "This is a big house with many rooms."

"I'll start while you get organized."

Steff gave up. "Go ahead."

Later, Paulie brought Steff an orange.

Steff asked, "Where did you find that?"

"In the refrigerator. I peeled it for you."

"You were looking for an artifact in the refrigerator?"

Paulie said, "Sort of."

Steff sighed. "This is a serious search, Paulie."

"I know." Paulie leaned close to Steff. "I don't want Jangles to get fired. He will feel awful."

Steff put her arm around Paulie. She guessed Paulie was remembering when their dad had been laid off from his job. Everyone in the family felt awful for a long time. Then Mom and Dad had started the business.

When Trigg and Reef came after lunch, the search team began to search the grounds of the estate.

The search went well, except Paulie kept running off to pick up rocks.

And walking around without finding anything important wasn't much fun for anyone.

Paulie's face turned pink. "I'm hot. Can we please stop for a while?"

They rested under a tree and drank from their water bottles.

Paulie polished her rocks with a tissue.

Trigg yawned. "I guess we should head home, Reef."

Reef said, "Right."

"Wait," Steff cried. Half of the search team was leaving. Four people could cover more ground than two. She had better give them the real reason for the search. "You guys like Jangles, don't you?"

"Sure," Trigg said.

"If I tell you something, promise not to tell

anyone? It might embarrass Jangles. Promise?"

Trigg and Reef nodded.

Steff lowered her voice. "The real reason we are looking for this artifact is to help Jangles keep his job."

She told them about Mr. Franklin and the History Group coming on Saturday.

"There will be a ceremony and everything," said Paulie.

Trigg whistled. "Big trouble for Jangles."

Reef said, "I'll look longer if Trigg will."

Paulie gathered up her rocks. Her face was still pink from the heat.

Trigg told her, "Here, I'll carry your rocks."

Much later, the search team still had not found anything.

The boys went home.

The girls dragged themselves toward the house.

Steff helped Paulie carry her rocks.

Near the house, the girls walked through a place where plants and vines grew wild.

Steff said, "No one has done yard work here for a long time."

"I'm tired." Paulie plopped down on a thick mat of vines. "Ouch! That dirt is hard." She moved to one side.

Under the leaves and branches, Steff saw concrete. "That's not dirt. Those vines have grown right over a sidewalk. Plants sure *do* grow well around here."

After a while, Paulie said, "Let's go."

She stood and took one step. Her foot broke through the tangle of vines and disappeared.

"That hurt!" she cried. "I stepped off the edge of the sidewalk."

Steff helped Paulie up.

"Strange," Steff muttered. "A sidewalk that doesn't go anywhere."

6

the water clue

Steff and Paulie spent the next morning checking the extra bedrooms for clues.

Trigg and Reef came right after lunch.

Hours later, everyone grew tired and sprawled in the shade.

Trigg pulled out his list of clues. "I have read these a dozen times."

Paulie said, "I don't know anything about the history of the Islands."

Steff turned to the boys. "You guys live here. What about the history?"

Trigg said, "Missionaries came."

"Whaling ships stopped at the Islands," added Reef. "Other ships brought things to sell."

"Steff and I flew here on an airplane," Paulie said.

Reef told her, "Before there were airplanes, people had to come on ships or boats."

"I guess much of our history has to do with water," said Trigg.

"Water!" Steff exclaimed. "I forgot to write one clue."

"About water?" asked Trigg.

"Yes. Mr. Franklin said the History Group will display the artifact near the ocean. He liked that. Said his artifact should be near water."

A funny look came over Trigg's face.

He said, "Water . . . fishing. Maybe Mr. Franklin plans to give away something old and special that has to do with fishing."

Paulie cried, "Don't tell me we are hunting for a fishing pole!"

Reef laughed. "Yeah, right! A big, old, heavy fishing pole!"

Paulie giggled. "So heavy we need a crate to move it?"

Steff was serious. "Actually, the artifact could have something to do with fishing."

Suddenly, Trigg jumped up. "Reef! We have to leave. Now!"

"What's the hurry?" Reef demanded.

"Just come on," Trigg said crossly.

Trigg was already walking away. Reef ran after him.

"See you guys tomorrow," called Steff.

The boys did not answer.

Paulie asked, "Why did they run off? We were only talking about history. And water."

"And fishing," Steff remembered. "Trigg sure got upset when we talked about fishing."

She thought a moment. "Hmmm. I think those boys are keeping something secret."

7

Visitors on the Ceiling

That evening, Steff and Paulie sat on the porch with Jangles. The air was soft and warm.

He showed them how to use a special needle and string pink plumeria blossoms together to make a lei.

Suddenly, a surprise sound came from around the corner of the house.

Snap! Did a branch break?

Then came quick, brushing noises, like

someone or something moving through bushes.

Jangles whispered, "Girls, go inside and stay by Marsha."

After a while, Jangles came in.

"Well, now," he said cheerfully. "Old Jangles must be hearing things."

"We heard something, too," said Paulie.

Jangles ruffled her hair. "Probably a dog."

Steff and Paulie went to their room.

Steff sat on her bed. She reached for her backpack.

Suddenly, Paulie screamed and jumped on Steff's bed, shouting, "Up there! Up there!"

Something that looked like a little lizard with big feet clung to the ceiling light.

"What's that?" Steff cried.

Nearby, a second lizard-like creature hung upside down with its feet flat aginst the ceiling. It flipped around and began to move.

Steff yelled, "That thing is running across the ceiling!"

Paulie screamed again.

Marsha and Jangles burst into the room.

Paulie shouted, "Over there—on the wall!"

That one skittered behind a picture. Another darted across the top of the mirror. One perched on the windowsill.

"Unbelievable!" roared Jangles. "Where did all those geckos come from?"

Paulie grabbed Steff's pillow and leaped through the air to her own bed. She swung the pillow over the bedspread like a golf club. Something flew off the bed.

"Way to go, Paulie," Jangles cried.

He marched across the floor and swooped up Paulie. He carried her out to the living room sofa.

Steff dashed after them and climbed on the sofa, too.

Marsha tried to make the girls feel better. "Geckos are a kind of lizard. They won't hurt you. They are precious in Hawaii because they eat bugs."

Steff shivered. "Can't they stay outside and eat bugs?"

Paulie sniffled. "There were so many of them."

Marsha agreed. "That was a lot of geckos to find in one place. But I'm sure we frightened them away."

Jangles and Marsha took the girls back to their bedroom.

Jangles checked everywhere. "Not a gecko in sight."

Steff asked, "Why would our room suddenly be full of geckos?"

"It is odd," Marsha said as she fluffed the pillows. She flapped the sheets this way and that. "There are none on these beds now."

Marsha and Jangles left.

As soon as the light went out, Paulie told Steff, "I should probably get in bed with you."

It was a narrow bed.

Steff said, "There's not much room."

"Good. That means there is no space for geckos."

Steff scooted to one side. "OK."

After a while, Paulie said in a sleepy voice, "Now we can tell Trigg and Reef we have seen a gecko."

Steff looked toward the window. "Yes. Lots of them."

quitters

On the way to search the tractor shed the next morning, the girls met Trigg and Reef.

The boys rushed by, going toward the garden shack.

"See you after lunch," Steff called.

Trigg kept walking. "Sorry. We're busy this afternoon."

"OK," Steff hollered. "We'll see you tomorrow."

Reef turned and walked backward. "We're busy all week."

Paulie told Steff, "Well!"

"I'm glad we're not quitters like they are," said Steff.

In the shed, Paulie climbed on a tractor and stayed there.

"We're supposed to be searching." Steff moved a box.

"I am searching." Paulie twisted around on the tractor, peering in all directions.

"You're not looking for an artifact. You're looking for geckos."

"I can see everything from up here, and I don't see anything historical."

Steff tried to open a barrel. The lid stuck.

"Oh, well," she said. "There's nothing important here anyway. Let's go."

After lunch, Steff said, "Perhaps we should look in the house this afternoon. No use going outside when it is so hot. We might be missing important clues inside."

She turned on the ceiling fan in the library and settled in a chair with a book.

"I'll read, too," said Paulie.

"I'm not simply reading," Steff told her.

"I'm searching. This book is about whaling ships that came to the Islands. That's history."

Paulie found a book about clothing once worn in Hawaii. "Old clothes are history, too."

Steff said, "I suppose so."

Of course, they weren't going to find the artifact with Paulie looking at pictures of dresses.

Paulie said, "I forgot to tell you what Mom said on the phone. She bought T-shirts for us in Honolulu."

"Yours probably has geckos drawn all over it," Steff teased.

Paulie opened another book. "Wow! Look at the pictures of volcanos on this island."

"Marsha told me there are lava tubes on Mr. Franklin's land, over by the ocean," said Steff.

"What's a lava tube? I forgot."

Steff said, "Lava comes oozing down from a volcano. It's hot and soft—like a river of pudding."

"Yummy!"

"The outside lava begins to cool and hardens into a black crust. The inside is still warm. The pudding—I mean lava—keeps flowing through it. When the warm lava moves on, it leaves a hole inside the cooled crust. That's why they call it a lava tube. Some places the crust breaks away, and you can see the empty hole inside."

When Steff finished the whaling ship book, she found an old scrapbook.

In it were stories cut from magazines and newspapers. Some told of parties at Mr. Franklin's estate. There were pictures of chairs and other furniture. Steff guessed they might be pictures of furniture bought for this house.

Steff got tired of looking at the scrapbook. She sorted the FAX messages again.

She found a clue in one FAX that she had forgotten to write on the list. She added it. *Made in Europe.*

She thought the list looked messy. Search team clues should be neat. So, she copied it over.

She gazed out the window for a while.

"Hey," she told Paulie, "let's climb that big tree. We can see all around from up there. We'll still be searching."

They went outside.

"Know what, Paulie?" Steff said. "I wish Mr. Franklin had a swimming pool here."

"Me too."

"The hotel where Mom and Dad are staying has one—maybe two or three."

9

iN tHe Lava tube

After dinner, Paulie wanted to pick flowers. Steff was still hoping for an orchid lei.

Jangles said, "Take a walk. Might be orchids blooming along the driveway."

At the end of the driveway, the girls saw Trigg and Reef walking on the road.

Instead of stopping to talk, the boys walked faster. They turned off the road.

"Where are you going?" called Steff.

Trigg yelled, "Taking a shortcut."

The boys were almost running now.

"Hmmm," Steff told Paulie. "A shortcut to where? That land belongs to Mr. Franklin. Let's follow them."

"What?"

"It's OK," Steff said. "Jangles told us to take a walk. I want to find out what they are up to. Those boys know something they don't want to tell."

Paulie said, "It could be a secret about the artifact."

The girls followed Trigg and Reef along a rough path.

The path became more and more rough. There were few plants here. The girls picked their way, going over and around huge chunks of black rock.

The roar of the ocean grew louder.

Steff knew she and Paulie must stop soon if they were to get back to the house before dark.

All of a sudden, the girls couldn't see Trigg or Reef.

Ahead, a pale light flickered. It moved rapidly, like a flashlight. Another came on.

The girls crept toward the lights. They heard voices.

The lights faded away.

Steff and Paulie came to a black hole. It looked like the entrance to a cave.

"It's a lava tube," Steff whispered to Paulie.

Suddenly, lights appeared again inside the lava tube.

The girls scrambled behind a big rock.

Trigg and Reef came out of the lava tube.

The boys looked around. They walked toward the rock where the girls hid.

Paulie covered her face with her hands.

The boys came near.

Steff squeezed hard against the rock.

Footsteps shuffled along the other side of the rock. It seemed forever before Trigg and Reef finally passed by.

Paulie uncovered her face.

Steff said, "Let's see what's in that lava tube."

"Not me!" cried Paulie.

"Those boys have a secret. It could be about the artifact."

Paulie hung back. "I'm not going in there."

"Don't be selfish. Think of Jangles and his job."

"I'm not selfish. I'm scared."

They crept inside the black hole.

They took a few steps across the bumpy floor of the lava tube.

Steff held one hand in front of her. They took a few more steps.

Suddenly, something touched Steff's face. Something stringy. It caught in her hair. She tried to brush it off. It wrapped itself around her arms like a spider web.

"Stay back, Paulie!" Steff cried.

Paulie screamed, "Let's get out of here!"

That was exactly what Steff was trying to do.

She ducked and twisted and finally got away.

The girls ran from the lava tube and headed for the house.

10

ƒLaƧHiNₒ ƧiₒN

It was dark when Steff and Paulie hurried through the front door.

Steff hoped Jangles wouldn't be worried.

She could never explain to him what happened at the lava tube. She couldn't even explain it to herself.

Marsha looked up from her books and waved.

"Girls?" Jangles called from his office. "Find orchids?"

"No," Steff said.

"Bummer," said Jangles. "Hey, I need a break. Let's have ice cream."

Paulie whispered to Steff, "We didn't find any secrets about the artifact either."

The porch was Steff's favorite place on the estate. Sitting there at night with Paulie and Jangles was one of her favorite things to do.

She didn't even mind when he teased her. "No orchids, huh? I'm surprised you haven't made a list of all the flowers on the estate. Some sort of chart."

Steff teased back, "Now I know why you wear white jeans. You can spill vanilla ice cream and no one will guess."

Jangles laughed. "Hey, these are my manager clothes."

Paulie said, "Steff and I have been praying about your job."

"Thanks, girls. I know you've been working hard, too, trying to find the artifact."

Tears stung Steff's eyes. *Not working hard enough,* she thought. She had spent hours doing easy things. The list of clues did not need to be copied. She had climbed the tree for fun.

Paulie asked, "Cousin Jangles, are you scared about Saturday?"

"I don't feel very good about Saturday. But I try to remember that if God wants me in this job, this is where I'll stay." Jangles jabbed his spoon in his ice cream. "For now, I'm here, and I'm still doing the best job I can."

Steff asked, "Isn't it hard to keep doing your best when you know Mr. Franklin may make you leave?"

Jangles reached off the porch and picked a hibiscus blossom. He tucked it in Steff's hair.

"Sure it's hard. But I found a verse in the Bible in Galatians—Chapter 6, the ninth verse. It keeps flashing in my thoughts. Like one of those flashing signs on a pizza place."

"What does the sign say?" asked Steff.

" 'Let us not become weary in doing good, for at the proper time we will reap a harvest if we do not give up.' "

Paulie said, "A harvest? Like your vegetables?"

Jangles chuckled. "I think it can mean more than a harvest of crops."

"I do, too," said Steff.

Jangles smiled at her. "That flashing sign tells me, 'Do what pleases God the best you know how. Don't quit. When it's the proper time, God will take care of the harvest, whatever it is.'"

Paulie closed her eyes. When she opened them, she said, "That sign has a lot of words. I need a shorter sign."

Jangles laughed. "Here's one for you: 'Don't quit doing what pleases God.'"

Steff carried the ice cream dishes into the kitchen.

She had prayed about Jangles' job. She had organized the search team to find the artifact. She was pretty sure it pleased God for her to help Jangles.

Yes, she had begun to do good. But today she had gotten tired of doing it.

Steff scrubbed the ice cream dishes until they were clean.

She would not quit. She would search even harder for the artifact that would save Cousin Jangles' job.

11

Way to go, Jangles!

After breakfast the next morning, Steff and Paulie found Jangles in his office. The door was open.

At first, Steff thought he was speaking on the telephone.

But he was talking to himself. "You've got to 'fess up to Mr. Franklin that the artifact is not ready for the big doings. Why? Because you don't know what or where the artifact is."

Steff knocked. "Cousin Jangles?"

Jangles grinned, but it did not look like a happy grin.

Steff rushed over to the desk. "Please don't tell Mr. Franklin yet."

"Have to. Don't want him to get here tomorrow and be embarrassed in front of those important people."

"Maybe we'll find the artifact today," Paulie said. "We're going to look all day."

A FAX message lay on the desk. Steff saw Mr. Franklin's name.

She asked, "Does this have more clues?"

Jangles shook his head in dismay. "I'm still having trouble with the FAX machine. Only the second page printed. I'll never be good with gadgets."

"But you're good with gardens," Paulie reminded him.

The top line of the second page had only one word. *Anchor.*

The rest of the message was about tomato plants.

Steff said, "Anchor and tomatoes. You

would think he would talk about the ceremony tomorrow."

Jangles grabbed the FAX. "Well, now! That's interesting. Maybe, just maybe, Mr. Franklin *did* talk about the ceremony."

"Huh?" said Steff.

"Anchor." Jangles frowned and tapped the paper on the desk. "I remember!" he cried. "Anchor! The artifact has something to do with anchors."

He shot both arms in the air and shouted, "Way to go, Jangles!"

"Wow!" said Steff. "That's the best clue yet."

Paulie started for the door. "Let's look for anchors."

"Come back!" Steff grabbed a pencil and tablet. "We have to organize a new search. This will be a search for anchors."

The telephone rang. Jangles answered it.

Steff wrote *Anchor* across the top of the page.

She whispered to Paulie, "What do we think of when we think of anchors?"

Paulie perched on a chair. "Water."

"Good." Steff wrote it down.

"Boats." Paulie bounced in the chair.

Steff began writing that, too. But suddenly she looked up. "Bathtub!"

Paulie stopped bouncing. "What has a bathtub got to do with anchors?"

Jangles finished the telephone call. "What's this?"

"I saw a bathtub with anchors," said Steff. "In a scrapbook in the library."

Jangles jumped to his feet. "Unbelievable!"

"It was an old-fashioned tub," Steff said. "Not one that fastens to a wall. This tub sat on four feet."

"Why did it have an anchor?" asked Paulie.

"Unbelievable!" cried Jangles again.

"It didn't have a real anchor," Steff answered Paulie. "It was decorated with anchors. A row of little anchors ran all around the outside of the tub."

Jangles clapped his hand to his forehead. "Unbelievable! I know that bathtub."

Steff stared at Jangles. "You know the bathtub?"

"It's an old cast-iron tub. Someone built a design right into the iron sides. They must have wanted a fancy tub when they made that one."

"Did you see the picture in the scrapbook, too?" asked Steff.

"No. I've seen the tub. The real tub."

"*The* tub?"

"Where?" asked Paulie.

"Outside," Jangles said. "Used to have flowers planted in it."

Steff said, "Anchors! We have found the artifact."

"Goodie!" squealed Paulie.

Jangles plopped in his chair and whirled all the way around. A big smile spread across his face.

"Cool!" he said.

12

clue review

The tub was nearly hidden by ferns growing in front of it. Branches hung over it. Floppy weeds grew bigger than the flowers inside it.

Steff pushed ferns out of the way.

"There's the row of anchors!" Paulie cried.

Steff read the clues again.

"Should be dry and clean."

The tub really needed cleaning. She put a check mark by that clue.

"Heavy. Needs strong crate for trip to town."

"That's for sure," said Jangles.

"*Old. Been on estate many years.*"

"Right," said Jangles.

"*Useful for school field trips.*"

Steff frowned. "Seems strange, but I guess it could be." She made a check mark.

"*Should be displayed near water.*"

Paulie said, "It used to have water in it."

"OK." Steff checked off the water clue and read the next. "*Made in Europe.*"

Jangles said, "Marsha says almost all the old furniture in the house came from Europe. She knows about old furniture."

Steff checked off the made-in-Europe clue.

"Any more clues?" asked Paulie.

There was one, but Steff wanted to forget it.

Jangles fingered his beads. They jingled softly. "Read the one about history."

Steff read, "*Played important part in history of the Islands.*"

"Oh," Paulie said sadly.

"Bummer," said Jangles.

"Hey!" Steff rapped her pencil on the tub. "This has to be the artifact. It has anchors and it's old and—"

"This may be old," said Jangles. "But how could a bathtub be important in the history of the Islands?"

Steff thought. "Maybe it was the first bathtub on this island."

"Could be," Paulie said hopefully.

"Maybe it is the only tub ever decorated with anchors."

"Possible," said Jangles.

"Besides," said Steff, "I read that important visitors to the island stayed in this house. Maybe a king from a faraway country took a bath in this very bathtub."

Steff wrote a big, black check mark by the history clue.

Paulie clapped.

Jangles ran his fingers through his hair. He boomed, "Well, how about that?" He answered himself. "Unbelievable!"

Jangles left for the workshop to build a crate.

The girls emptied the tub and cleaned it the best they could.

That night, Jangles and the girls sat on the

porch and ate bowls of vanilla ice cream.

Jangles laughed a lot.

Marsha put away her books and came outside, too. She hugged Jangles again and again.

They made leis to give to the History Group.

Paulie giggled so much that she spilled chocolate sauce on Jangles' white jeans.

"No biggie," he said. "I can go wash them in that clean, heavy, historical bathtub."

Marsha pretended to push him off the porch.

Steff felt warm inside. Tonight she hardly minded that Mom and Dad were in Honolulu while she and Paulie were here on the Big Island of Hawaii.

The next morning, Marsha had to go to a Saturday class at her school.

Jangles left to meet Mr. Franklin at the airport.

The girls straightened up the kitchen.

A knock sounded at the door.

cast-iron Message

Trigg and Reef stood on the front porch.

Trigg jammed his hands in his pockets. He said, "We came to say we are sorry about quitting your search team."

Reef added, "And about the way we acted."

The girls stepped outside.

Trigg looked uncomfortable. "We . . . we had a reason."

Reef said, "Yeah, we wanted to get rid of you."

Trigg punched Reef's arm. "What he means

is, we wanted you to stop searching for the artifact."

"Why?" asked Steff.

"We were afraid you would find something we have," explained Reef.

Trigg said, "Remember our club? We call it the Net Club."

"So?"

"We have a big, very old net. It once was used for fishing. We found it at the beach. When we heard the clue about the artifact having to do with water, we were afraid our net might be your artifact."

Paulie said, "Your net can't be our—"

"Tell us more about your net!" Steff broke in.

Trigg said, "It's hanging in our clubhouse."

Steff remembered something. "You mean hanging like a big, stringy spider web?"

"I guess so," Trigg said.

"Where is your clubhouse?" she demanded.

Reef said quickly, "That's a secret."

Steff winked at Paulie.

Paulie cupped her hands around her mouth

and leaned close to Steff's ear. "In the lava tube."

Steff told the boys, "Jangles is on his way to meet Mr. Franklin."

"We better go get the net," said Trigg.

Reef said sadly, "The Net Club won't be much of a club without its net."

Steff realized the boys were giving up something that was important to them. They were giving it up to help Jangles.

Of course, the net was not the artifact at all. The tub, decorated with anchors, was the artifact.

She and Paulie burst into laughter.

Steff asked Paulie, "Shall we show them?"

Paulie giggled.

"Show us what?" demanded Trigg.

"Come on," Steff yelled.

She and Paulie dashed off the porch and ran toward the tub.

She was glad the boys did not have to give up their net.

"See!" Paulie cried. "Here is the artifact. We found it yesterday."

Trigg and Reef stared at the tub.

Trigg said, "But our net fits the clues. Heavy. Old. Water. Fishing has always been important to the Islands."

Reef said, "It was probably made here on the estate."

Steff said, "Yesterday, we got a new clue. We learned that the artifact had to do with anchors."

Paulie showed them the row of anchors around the tub.

Trigg squatted down and studied it.

"Besides," said Paulie. "You said your net was probably made on this island. The artifact was made in Europe."

Trigg crawled around to the end of the tub.

"Hey!" he called. "If the artifact was made in Europe, this bathtub is not the artifact."

Steff scrambled to see where Trigg was looking.

He pointed to something written in the cast iron. The letters had been formed when the tub was made.

"You must have missed seeing this," he said.

Steff rubbed her fingers over the letters. The words read *Made in U.S.A.*

Steff wanted to cry.

Trigg was right.

The tub had not come with the other furniture from Europe. It had not come from Europe at all.

The tub was not the artifact.

14

our ſearch team
never quitſ

Steff leaned against the bathtub—the silly old bathtub. She and Paulie had tried and tried to help Jangles. She was tired of trying. Weary.

Then Steff remembered the verse Jangles had talked about—the one he said kept flashing in his thoughts like a sign.

It began, *Let us not become weary in doing good. . . .*

Steff jumped to her feet.

"We are not giving up!" she declared.

She ran into the house and brought out the map.

Paulie said, "While you look at the map, I know what I'll do." She hurried toward the garden shack.

Steff tried to make a plan. Jangles would return soon with Mr. Franklin.

Paulie left the garden shack carrying tools. She stopped near some small plants with red blossoms. She called, "I'll dig up these flowers and move them where they will show."

"That's nice," Reef called back. But it sounded as if he was almost laughing.

Paulie started digging. "I don't care what you think. If Mr. Franklin likes the way the estate looks, he may not be so angry."

Steff said, "You go ahead, Paulie. It will be pretty."

Reef said, "Guess it can't hurt."

Steff studied the map. "Water! The artifact is tied to water. How?"

Trigg said, "When I think of water, I think of ocean. A glass of water." He chuckled. "Of course, I think of a bathtub."

"Rain," said Steff.

"Swimming," said Trigg. "A swimming pool."

They heard Paulie calling, "Can somebody help me? This dirt is hard."

Trigg asked, "Reef, would you help her? We're working on a plan."

Reef said, "OK. Until there's something important to do."

Steff said, "Where were we? Oh yes, a swimming pool. Well, there's no pool on this estate."

"Used to be," said Trigg.

"Huh?"

"My grandfather told me he used to swim here."

Reef had gone to help Paulie. He yelled, "Paulie's right about this dirt. It's as hard as concrete."

"Hey," Steff exclaimed. "You're digging where Paulie and I found an old sidewalk. Remember, Paulie?" she called. "You stepped through the vines?"

Suddenly, Steff grabbed the map. She

looked over at Paulie and Reef. Then she looked back at the map.

Paulie was standing where the big circle was drawn on the map. They thought the circle might have been a large flower bed.

But they were wrong. The circle had been drawn to show a swimming pool in that spot.

The sidewalk that ended wasn't a sidewalk at all. It was part of the concrete deck around a swimming pool—a pool that hadn't been used for a long time.

Steff dropped the map and ran toward Paulie and Reef. "That's an old swimming pool covered over by vines and weeds!" she shouted. "A pool would have been filled with water."

Trigg raced up and started tearing away plants. "And water might lead us to the artifact."

Using garden tools and their hands, they worked as quickly as they could.

They pulled up plants and dug through dirt. They threw out dead branches.

They discovered a concrete post standing in the pool.

Trigg felt its jagged top. "Something broke off of this."

"It will take days to clear out the whole pool," Reef said.

Steff tugged on a vine. She would not give up. She pulled and pulled.

The vine snapped. She threw it aside and bent down to get the rest of it.

But it was growing around something near the bottom of the pool.

Something big and heavy.

Her heart raced.

"Help me!" she cried.

Nearly hidden in a tangle of roots was an anchor. A ship's anchor.

They had found the artifact.

Near the house, a car honked.

"It must be Jangles!" said Steff.

Paulie squealed, "And Mr. Franklin. What should we do?"

"Quick," said Steff. "Paulie, you go meet them. Tell Jangles he is needed here. You keep Mr. Franklin at the house."

Paulie's eyes opened wide. "How?"

"I don't know," Steff said. "Give him a lei."

"Show him the window where the geckos got into your room," said Reef.

Trigg sent Reef a strange look.

Paulie ran.

Later, Steff was knocking dirt from her shoes when she heard Paulie's voice.

"I hope you like your lei, Mr Franklin."

A man answered, "It is the nicest one I've seen, Paulie."

Steff knew Paulie had kept Mr. Franklin away as long as she could.

But everything was OK now.

With Jangles' help, they had pulled the anchor from the swimming pool and cleaned it off.

The anchor must have toppled from the concrete post long before.

Now it lay on a bed of fresh, green palm leaves, ready for Mr. Franklin to give to the History Group.

Jangles said, "Here it is, Mr. Franklin."

Mr. Franklin smiled at everyone.

He said, "This anchor was on the first ship

my family owned. It made many trips between the Islands. Good job."

Jangles said, "Thank you." He winked at the search team.

Steff and the others walked toward the house.

Trigg said, "Reef and I had better go."

"Please stay," Paulie said. "You helped find the artifact."

Steff said, "Yes. Let's climb that big tree in the yard. We'll watch the ceremony from there."

She grinned and added, "While we are waiting, you can tell us what you know about geckos getting into our room."

"Hey!" Trigg laughed. "We just sort of helped them through the window. Just to scare you a little."

Reef said, "We wanted you to quit searching so you wouldn't find our net."

Both girls giggled as they ran for the tree and started to climb.

The boys followed.

Steff found a good place to sit. She shouted down, "You mean you didn't want us to find